KU-300-759

or

Iris Howden

Published in association with
The Basic Skills Agency

Hodder & Stoughton

A MEMBER OF THE HODDER HEADLINE GROUP

Acknowledgements
Cover: Mark Preston
Illustrations: Chris Coady

Orders: please contact Bookpoint Ltd, 130 Milton Park, Abingdon, Oxon OX14
4SB. Telephone: (44) 01235 827720, Fax: (44) 01235 400454. Lines are open from
9.00–6.00, Monday to Saturday, with a 24 hour message answering service. You
can also order through our website: www.hodderheadline.co.uk.

British Library Cataloguing in Publication Data
A catalogue record for this title is available from The British Library

ISBN 0 340 87668 9

First published 2003
Impression number 10 9 8 7 6 5 4 3 2 1
Year   2007 2006 2005 2004 2003

Typeset by SX Composing DTP, Rayleigh, Essex.
Printed in Great Britain for Hodder & Stoughton Educational, a division of
Hodder Headline, 338 Euston Road, London NW1 3BH by Athenaeum Press,
Gateshead, Tyne and Wear.

Contents

1
Trick or Treat

'No,' Danny's mum said. 'No way!
You are not playing Trick or Treat.
And that's final.'

'But Mum,' Danny stopped there.
He knew better than to argue
when his mum was in that mood.

But his mum had more to say.
'Some of the old people I work for
are scared stiff at Halloween,' she said.
'They don't want to open the door to kids
dressed as ghosts and witches.'

Danny's mum worked as a home help.
She knew a lot of old people.

Danny thought she was making
a fuss about nothing.
Trick or Treat was only a bit of fun.
Nobody got hurt, did they?

He said this to his best mate, Jono.
'Take no notice,' Jono said.
'You know what mothers are like!
She'll change her mind.'

Danny shook his head.
'You don't know my mum,' he said.

'Come out anyway,' Jono said.
'You can make up some excuse.
Say you're going to the library.'

'As if!' Danny said.
'When do we ever go to the library?'

'There's always a first time,' Jono said.
He never let things worry him.
'Let's go down to the joke shop,'
he said, 'and buy the gear.
You can leave yours at my house.'

The two lads had a great time.
They tried on all the masks.
Jono put on a pair of hairy hands.
'I like these,' he said.
'Watch out for the werewolf.
Ow-oo, ow-oo,' he began to howl.

'Stop mucking about,' the shop owner said.
'Do you want to buy anything or not?'

Back at Jono's house
they tipped out the bag.
Jono had bought a skeleton outfit.
There was a skull mask,
and a set of paper bones.
'These glow in the dark,' Jono said.

'I'll wear my black jumper and jeans.
Pin these on. I'll look quite spooky.'

Danny laughed. 'Great,' he said.
'What do you think of my vampire kit?
Scary, or what?'
He slicked his hair back with gel.
Then he fitted plastic fangs
over his teeth.
Last he tied a black cape
around his neck.

'Help!' Jono fell about, holding his neck.
'I'm scared to death.
Please don't bite me, Count Danny.
I'm too young to die.'

'It'll look better with make-up,' Danny said.
'A white face. Red rims round my eyes.'

'And fake blood,' Jono added.
'Don't forget to use plenty of blood.'

2
Halloween

It was Halloween night.
Danny looked out of the window.
At seven o'clock, it was dark already.
All the lads would be out having fun.
He was stuck indoors like a little kid.
The phone rang.
His mother went to answer it.

'That was your sister Linda,' she said.
'She's been invited to a party.
She wants me to babysit.
I won't be back till after midnight.
Dad should be home soon.
Tell him his dinner's in the microwave.'

Danny watched TV for a while.

He dared not sneak out.

His dad might come home at any minute.

The phone rang again.

It was his dad. He was in a hurry.

'Tell your mother I've got to work late,'

he told Danny.

He rang off

before Danny could say anything.

Danny could not believe his luck.

Both his parents would be out for hours.

He ran over to Jono's house.

'You made it. Good man,' Jono said.

'Come in and get dressed up.'

He had his skeleton outfit on.

It looked quite scary in the dark hall.

'Hurry up. It's getting late.'

He picked up his backpack.

'What's in there?' Danny asked.

Jono showed him a large torch.
He also had a tin with a string
tied to it as a handle.
'This is to put the cash in,' he said.

It was a cold dark night.
The two lads went round,
knocking on doors.
Ringing bells.
Some people did not answer.
Some told them to go away.
One or two gave them sweets.
Only a few gave them money.
Small coins, like 10 or 20 pence pieces.

'This is a waste of time,' Jono said.

'Let's go home,' Danny said.
'My feet are freezing.'

'We'll finish this street,' Jono said.
'Then we'll stop.'

They came to the last house.
Jono rang the bell.
A little old man came to the door.
'Yes,' he said. 'What do you want?'

Jono rattled the tin under his nose.
'Trick or treat?' he asked.

'Go away!' the old man told him.
'I'm not giving you money.
This is just begging.'

'It's only a bit of fun,' Jono said.
'Weren't you ever young, mister?'

'Don't be cheeky,' the man said.
'Now clear off, or I'll call my son.'

3
The Chase

Danny was halfway down the path.
He looked round and saw Jono
take something from his backpack.
'What are you doing?' he asked.
'He said he'd call his son.'

'He can call the *army* out
for all I care!' Jono said.
He had an egg box in his hand.
He opened it and took out an egg.

'Don't!' Danny shouted.
'Come on, let's go.'

'Don't be such a wuss,' Jono said.
He took aim and threw an egg
at the front window.
He laughed as it went splat
against the glass.
The yellow mess ran down the pane.

The front door burst open.
This time, it was not the old man.
A large young man filled the doorway.
He looked very fit.
The sort who spent time at the gym.
'Just you wait, you little devils,'
he shouted.
'I'll give you Trick or Treat!'

'Run for it,' Jono shouted,
but Danny didn't need to be told.
Danny was off up the road as fast
as he could go.
He heard Jono coming up behind him.

Jono was a really good runner.
He could always beat Danny in a race.
'See you later!' Jono shouted,
as he sped past.

Danny began to panic.
He was getting tired.
Soon the young man would catch him.
Danny didn't want to get the blame
for what Jono had done.

He ran round a corner.
There were no streetlights there.
He was passing the old church.
Danny saw his chance and took it.
He ran into the graveyard
and hid behind a gravestone.

With a bit of luck, the man had not seen him.
He lay there puffing and panting.
Out of breath after the chase.

4
A Night of Horror

Danny lay looking up at the sky.
Black clouds moved across a full moon.
It gave a lot of light.
Danny could see quite well.
He got up from the cold damp earth
and looked around.

Across the graveyard, someone was moving.
It looked like a skeleton.
Jono must have come to find him.
They often met in the churchyard.
It was a good place to hide.

The figure began to dance about.
It waved its bony arms and legs.
Danny laughed.
'Just like Jono,' he thought.
'Acting the fool.
That skeleton outfit looks pretty good.
Very realistic in this light.
You could take it for a real one.'
He got up and ran across the churchyard.

As he got near to the skeleton,
Danny began to feel afraid.
This was not Jono winding him up.
He could see right through the bones.
Suddenly he felt cold all over.
This skeleton was for real!

Quickly, he turned to run away.
Another skeleton came up behind him.
Then another, and another.
More skeletons came out
from behind the graves.

They formed a ring around him.
Danny's mouth went dry.
His heart began to thump.
He stood, frozen to the spot with fear.

The skeletons moved in on him.
Bony hands took hold of his.
They pulled him into the circle.
Skulls nodded at him.
Clack, clack, clack.
Bony feet began to beat out a rhythm.
The circle broke.
The line of skeletons,
with Danny in the middle,
began to dance.
They pulled him along,
weaving in and out of the gravestones.

Their feet clicked over the gravel paths.
Click, click, click.
Their bony arms and legs rattled.
Clatter, clatter, clatter.

The dry bones shaking and swinging
made an awful noise.

Danny twisted and turned.
He tried to pull his hands
out of their grip.
The skeletons held on tight.
They jerked him along,
moving faster and faster.
Danny's vampire fangs fell out.
His cloak was ripped apart.
His hair fell in his eyes
so he could not see.

He got hotter and hotter.
Soon he was worn out,
gasping for breath.
His arms ached from being pulled along.
He screamed in terror.
It made no difference.
The horrible dance went on and on.
Then he blacked out.

5
Home at Last!

He came to with Jono bending over him.
'Wake up,' he was saying. 'Speak to me.'

Danny opened his eyes.
'What happened?' he asked.

'You must have fallen over,'
Jono told him.
'You've cut your head.'

Danny put his hand up to his forehead.
It was wet with blood.

'Come on,' Jono said.
'Let's get you home.'
He helped Danny to his feet.
Danny held on to Jono's arm.
He felt very weak.
It was an effort to walk.
He looked around the churchyard.
It was empty.
There was no one in sight.

Slowly they walked to Danny's house.
'Goodnight, Jono,' Danny said.
'And thanks. See you in the morning.'
He shut the front door
and went up to the bathroom.

He looked into the mirror.
His face was a mess.
He scrubbed at it with a flannel.
He washed off the make-up.
He washed off the fake blood.
It was mixed with the real thing.

Quickly he got ready for bed.
His hands shook
as he took off his clothes.
His jeans were torn.
His shirt was filthy.
His trainers were thick with mud.
He was shaking so much
that he had to sit for a moment
on the bathroom floor.

Danny put on his pyjamas
and went to bed.
He switched off the light
and pulled the duvet over his head.

The last thing he heard
before he fell asleep
was his dad's car in the drive.

6
A History Lesson

Next day on the school bus, Jono said,
'You look white as a sheet. Are you OK?'

'Fine,' Danny said, but he wasn't.
He felt ill. His arms and legs hurt.
He had a really bad headache.

Danny had not slept well.
He kept having nightmares.
In daylight, he thought
he must have dreamed the whole thing.
He couldn't really have been in a dance
with skeletons, could he?
That fall had made him imagine it all.

Their first class was History.
They were learning about the Middle Ages.
Jono picked up the handout from the desk.
'The Black Death,' it said at the top.
'This looks more interesting,' Jono said.

'Settle down,' said Miss Wilson.
'Who can tell me how the plague
came to England?'

'Please, Miss.'
This was Mandy, the class swot.
'Rats came ashore off the ships.
They brought fleas with them.
People got bitten and caught the plague.'

'Good,' Miss Wilson said.
'That's right, Mandy.'

Jono made scratching noises under his desk.
'Squeak, squeak, squeak,' he said.
He ran his fingers up and down the back
of the girl in front of him.
'It's a big rat,' he said.
'Coming to bite you.'
She screamed.

'Come out and sit here,'
Miss Wilson told Jono.
'Just behave yourself.'

Jono took his books
and moved to the front.
'Turn to the next page,' the teacher said.

Danny turned over his work-sheet.
He looked at it in horror.
The photocopy was dark.
It was not very clear.
But he knew at once what it was.

It was a picture of a line of skeletons.
They were holding hands.

Danny shut his eyes.
He could hear it all again.
The sound of bony feet tapping.
Click, click, click.
The rattle of bony arms.
Clatter, clatter, clatter.
The awful sound the dry bones had made . . .
He knew it had been for real.

'Does anyone know
what this picture is about?'
Miss Wilson asked.
Mandy's hand shot up again.
Danny heard her answer.
It seemed to come from a long way away.

'Please, Miss,' she said.
'It's called the Dance of Death.'